SUNBEAM

WRITTEN BY WANDA WYONT

ILLUSTRATED BY SUZIE HUSKINS

Parkway Publishers, Inc.
Boone, North Carolina

available from:
Parkway Publishers, Inc.
Post Office Box 3678
Boone, North Carolina 28607
www.parkwaypublishers.com
Tel/Fax: (828) 265-3993

Library of Congress Cataloging-in-Publication Data

Wyont, Wanda.
  Sunbeam / by Wanda Wyont ; [Suzie Huskins, illustrations].
     p. cm.
  Summary: Kim is immediately enchanted by the beautiful golden
horse that is delivered to her home, then disappointed to learn
that he is intended for another girl with the same last name as
Kim. Includes multidisciplinary teaching strategies.
  ISBN 1-933251-07-7
[1. Horses--Fiction.] I. Huskins, Suzanne Hallier, ill. II.
Title.
  PZ7.W9936Su 2005
  [E]--dc22

  2005007988

Book design by Aaron Burleson, spokesmedia

For my husband Garry
and daughter, Kim

— Wanda

I first met Sunbeam when he was delivered to my house! I did not know it at the time, but he would change my life. It had been an ordinary day. My cousin, Christopher, and I had been playing Wild West all afternoon. We had spent the day galloping around on our stick horses.

I was wearing my red cowgirl hat, a pair of red boots, and a vest with brown fringe on it. Christopher had on his black cowboy hat, a Texas Ranger scarf, and a sheriff's badge that was pinned onto his shirt.

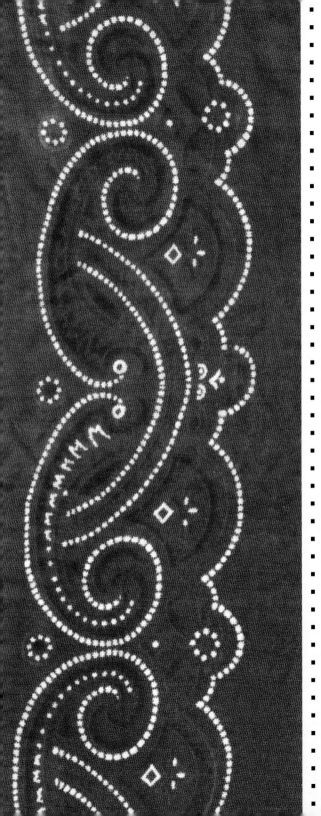

Our legs were tired and we had climbed up into one of our favorite spots: the Shade Tree. It was a large oak tree at the end of the long driveway. It had low branches so we could climb up the tree and shimmy out on the limb that hung over the road.

We sat quietly and dangled our legs. I could see our stick horses propped against the tree beneath us. I rode an old broom from my grandmother's kitchen; I pretended that it was a golden palomino. Christopher said his horse was solid black.

2

We heard a rattling noise coming down the road. It wasn't the sound of a car. We turned our heads at the same time and saw a red truck pulling a trailer.

The truck turned down our driveway and passed under us. There was a horse in the trailer just below our feet. Christopher and I scrambled down the tree and ran toward the house. When we got there, the horse was being unloaded from the trailer and the driver of the truck was talking to my grandfather.

It was then that I got a surprise. "Do you live here?" asked the other man.

"Yes," I answered, wondering what he meant.

"Well, then, I am delivering Sunbeam to you," he said.

Sunbeam was a tall horse with a golden coat and white stockings and mane. He held his head high and proud. He stood perfectly still.

The man began putting on Sunbeam's saddle and bridle. When he finished, he asked, "Do you wanna ride him?" I nodded and walked toward the horse.

As the man lifted me onto Sunbeam's back, I could see my mother coming out of the house and walking toward my grandfather. I waved at them as I was being led down the driveway.

I had never ridden a real horse. My heart was racing! I was sitting higher than the hedge by the driveway. Sunbeam neighed and shook his head as he walked along on the sandy road. I stroked his mane with one hand and held on tightly with the other hand. I felt his strength as I gently moved back and forth. I knew I wasn't dreaming, but it was like a dream.

When the man turned us around and headed back toward the house, I could see that Mother looked worried. I nervously rubbed Sunbeam's golden coat.

When I got within earshot, I heard some of Mother's questions. "Who bought this horse? When was it purchased?"

"Bob Grigg called my barn yesterday and told us to deliver this horse to his daughter, Kim," the man said.

Bob Grigg is my dad's name, so I waited to see what would happen next.

"May I see your delivery slip?" Mother continued, still not convinced.

My mother studied the form and then glanced at me before saying, "I'm sorry, you have the wrong address! This says Highway 18 and we are off Stage Coach Road. It is unusual to have two families with the same name in this small community, but there is a Grigg family that owns a large horse stable outside of Fallston."

I could barely hear the driver's apology. All I could think of was that I had lost my horse!

After giving Christopher a ride, the men loaded up Sunbeam and left. I stood and silently watched the trailer disappear down the driveway. My mother hugged me and said, "I am so sorry!"

That night, Mother came into my bedroom to tuck me in, but instead of a story, we talked about Sunbeam. "I wanted the horse and you sent him away," I cried.

Mother said, "It is okay to feel sad." After that, I started feeling better.

The next day, our family took a drive to the Grigg Equestrian Stables on Highway 18. After parking, Dad got out and Mother and I stayed in the car. Later, Dad appeared in the doorway and motioned for us to join him. As we went into the large barn, I saw many different horses. Some were in their stalls and I could only see their heads peeking out into the barn.

Other horses were being ridden around an arena that was inside of the large barn. It only took a quick look to spot Sunbeam. He was saddled and waiting for someone to ride him.

"Welcome to my barn," said the man standing with my dad. "I am Mr. Grigg," he added, looking at me. "I believe that you have already met Sunbeam," he said, glancing toward the palomino. As I looked toward the horse, an older girl was mounting him.

I was captured by the sight and sounds of the arena when Mr. Grigg said, "He is a champion American Saddlebred, and my daughter is a wonderful rider." Then he smiled down at me and asked, "Kim, how would you like to learn to ride like that? I have lots of horses that would be perfect."

Sunbeam pranced around the arena inside the barn. He lifted his legs high as the rider bobbed up and down. I was watching the exhibition. Sunbeam cantered around the sandy circle.

My parents smiled. I nodded toward Mr. Grigg and he called instructions to a stable boy: "Tim, saddle up Buttercup and bring him over here." In a few minutes, a spotted horse was led over to where we stood. After a short lesson on how to use the reins, I got a leg up into the saddle. While my parents watched, I rode the horse out to a small ring with Tim walking beside me.

Buttercup was a gentle horse. He seemed content to walk slowly around and around the small ring. I held onto the reins and tugged slightly when I wanted him to turn. With each new lap, I felt more at ease. By the time my first lesson was over, I knew that I loved riding.

Before leaving the barn that Saturday, I told Mr. Grigg that I would like to learn to ride like his daughter. He smiled and said if I was willing to put in the hard work, he would have me riding champion horses someday. I smiled and thought, "It may even be Sunbeam!"

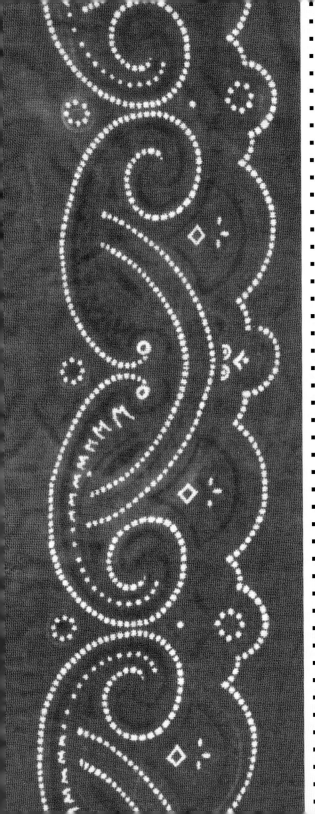

Teaching Strategies

Literacy and Language Development
Ask the following questions after the book has been read.
1. Who are the main characters in the story?
2. Where did the story take place?
3. What are the differences in Kim and Christopher's pretend horses?
4. What happened first in the story? Second?
5. What do you think will happen after Kim learns to ride?

Discuss Feelings
1. Have you ever felt sad?
2. Have you ever felt angry?
3. What things can you do when you feel sad or angry?

Creative Activities
1. Draw a picture of a horse, barn, stable, etc.
2. Create a new ending to this story.

Physical Movement

1. Try to ride on a pretend horse (discarded broom).

Math Concepts
1. Match, sort, and classify different plastic horses, figures, hats, etc.

Science Concepts
1. Visit a horse stable.
2. How would you take care of a horse?